POLLYANNA

ELEANOR H. PORTER

CONDENSED AND ADAPTED BY
LAURA HILL

ILLUSTRATED BY
JON SAYER

COVER ILLUSTRATED BY
JERRY DILLINGHAM

Dalmatian 🐾 Press

The Dalmatian Press Children's Classics Collection
has been adapted and illustrated with care and thought,
to introduce you to a world of famous authors, characters, ideas,
and great stories that have been loved for generations.

Editor — Kathryn Knight
Creative Director — Gina Rhodes
And the entire classics project team of Dalmatian Press

ALL ART AND ADAPTED TEXT © DALMATIAN PRESS, LLC

ISBN: 1-57759-539-4 mass
1-57759-561-0 base

First Published in the United States in 2003 by Dalmatian Press, LLC, USA

Copyright © 2003 Dalmatian Press, LLC

Printed and bound in the U.S.A.

The DALMATIAN PRESS name and logo are
trademarks of Dalmatian Press, LLC, Franklin, Tennessee 37067.

11391

03 04 05 06 07 LBM 10 9 8 7 6 5 4 3 2 1

A note to the reader—

A classic story rests in your hands. The characters are famous. The tale is timeless.

This Dalmatian Press Children's Classic has been carefully condensed and adapted from the original version (which you really *must* read when you're ready for every detail). We kept the well-known phrases for you. We kept the author's style. And we kept the important imagery and heart of the tale.

Literature is terrific fun! It encourages you to think. It helps you dream. It is full of heroes and villains, suspense and humor, adventure and wonder, and new ideas. It introduces you to writers who reach out across time to say: "Do you want to hear a story I wrote?"

Curl up and enjoy.

DALMATIAN PRESS
ILLUSTRATED CLASSICS

CONTENTS

CHARACTERS

POLLYANNA WHITTIER — a lonely but cheerful eight-year-old orphan girl who comes to live with her spinster Aunt Polly

MISS POLLY HARRINGTON (AUNT POLLY) — the stern older sister of Pollyanna's mother, not at all sure she's ready to care for a child

NANCY — Aunt Polly's hard-working housemaid, and Pollyanna's soft-hearted friend

JOHN PENDLETON — a crabby, mysterious neighbor who finds he needs Pollyanna

DR. THOMAS CHILTON — a kindly doctor who changes Pollyanna's life in several ways

MRS. SNOW — an invalid neighbor lady who learns from Pollyanna the importance of being glad

MILLY — Mrs. Snow's daughter

OLD TOM — Aunt Polly's gardener

JIMMY BEAN — a little boy who finds a friend in a fellow orphan

DR. WARREN — the doctor who is called to attend to Pollyanna

WIDOW TARBELL AND MRS. BENTON — two of the many visitors who express well wishes for Pollyanna

POLLYANNA

CHAPTER ONE

Miss Polly

Miss Polly Harrington entered her kitchen a little hurriedly this June morning. Miss Polly did not usually hurry. She prided herself on her calm manner. But today she was actually hurrying.

Nancy, washing dishes at the sink, looked up in surprise. Nancy had been working in Miss Polly's kitchen only two months, but already she knew that her mistress did not usually hurry.

"Nancy!" Miss Polly called sternly.

"Yes, ma'am," Nancy answered cheerfully, wiping a pitcher in her hand.

"Nancy, when I'm talking to you, please stop your work and listen to what I have to say."

Nancy's face flushed. She set the pitcher down and nearly tipped it over, which made her even more nervous.

"Yes, ma'am, I will, ma'am," she stammered. "I was only keepin' on with my work 'cause you specially told me to hurry with my dishes."

Her mistress frowned.

"That will do, Nancy. I did not ask for explanations," Miss Polly said. "When you've finished, you may clear the little room at the head of the stairs in the attic, and make up the bed. Sweep the room and clean it, of course, after you clear out the trunks and boxes."

Miss Polly paused, then went on. "I suppose I may as well tell you now, Nancy. My niece, Miss Pollyanna Whittier, is coming to live with me. She is eleven years old, and will sleep in that room."

"A little girl—coming here, Miss Harrington? Oh, won't that be nice!" cried Nancy.

"Nice? Well, that isn't exactly the word I would use," said Miss Polly stiffly. "However, I intend to make the best of it. I am a good woman, and I know my duty. See that you clean the corners, Nancy," she finished sharply, as she left the room.

"Yes, ma'am," sighed Nancy.

In her own room, Miss Polly took out the letter she had received days before from a faraway Western town. It had been an unpleasant surprise to her. The letter was addressed to Miss Polly Harrington, Beldingsville, Vermont. It read:

Dear Madam:

I regret to inform you that the Rev. John Whittier died two weeks ago, leaving one child, a girl eleven years old. He left practically nothing else for the child except a few books. As you doubtless know, he was the pastor of this small mission church, and had a very small salary.

He had expressed that for your sister's sake you might wish to bring the child up with her own family in the East. If you can take her, we would appreciate it very much if you would telegram at once. A man and his wife here are going East very soon. They would take her with them to Boston and put her on the Beldingsville train. Of course you would be notified when to expect Pollyanna.

Hoping to hear from you soon, I remain,
Respectfully yours,
Jeremiah O. White.

With a frown, Miss Polly folded the letter and tucked it into its envelope. She had telegrammed saying she would take the child, of course. She *hoped* she knew her duty well enough for that!

As she sat, she thought about her older sister, Jennie, the child's mother. Jennie, as a girl of twenty, had insisted upon marrying the young minister. Her family had hoped she would marry another man who also loved her—a richer, older man. But Jennie loved the minister. So she married him and moved away to become a missionary.

Polly had been only fifteen when her sister moved away. The family had little more to do with Jennie. Jennie had written, for a time. She named her last baby "Pollyanna" for her two sisters, Polly and Anna. The other babies had all died. A few years after the child's birth, the minister wrote a little heartbroken note, telling them of Jennie's death.

"I'm glad I know my duty," thought Miss Polly as she climbed the stairs to the attic room. "But *Pollyanna*! What a ridiculous name!"

The room contained a small bed, neatly made, two straight-backed chairs, a washstand, a dresser with no mirror, and a small table. No curtains. No pictures. All day the sun had been pouring down, and the little room was like an oven. There were no screens on the closed windows. A big fly was buzzing angrily at a window, trying to get out.

"Nancy," Miss Polly said later downstairs, "I found a fly in Miss Pollyanna's room. I have ordered screens, but until they come I expect you to see that the windows remain closed. My niece will arrive tomorrow at four o'clock. Please meet her at the station. The telegram says 'light hair, red-checked gingham dress, and straw hat.' "

Promptly at twenty minutes to four the next afternoon, Timothy the handyman and Nancy drove off to meet the expected guest.

And there she stood at the station—a slender little girl in a red-checked gingham with two fat braids of golden hair hanging down her back. Beneath the straw hat, an eager, freckled little face turned right and left, plainly searching for someone. She was standing by herself when Nancy approached her.

"Are you Miss—Pollyanna?" Nancy asked. The next moment she found herself half smothered in two gingham-clad arms.

"Oh, I'm so glad, *glad*, GLAD to see you," cried an eager voice. "Of course I'm Pollyanna, and I'm so glad you came to meet me! I hoped you would."

"You—you did?" stammered Nancy, wondering how Pollyanna could possibly have known her.

"Oh, yes. I've been wondering all the way here what you looked like," cried the little girl, dancing on her toes. "And now I know, and I'm glad you look just like you do."

Pollyanna's words were very confusing to Nancy. She was relieved when Timothy came up and the three were off at last. Nancy was dazed by all the little girl's comments and questions.

"Is it far? I hope it is—I love to ride," sighed Pollyanna. "Of course, if it isn't far I won't mind, 'cause I'll be glad to get there all the sooner. What a pretty street! I *knew* it was going to be pretty. Father told me…" The girl paused, with tears in her eyes. Then she went on. "Oh, I ought to explain about this red gingham dress, you know, and why I'm not in black. Part of the Ladies' Aid wanted to buy me a black dress and hat, but the other part thought the money ought to go toward the red carpet for the church, you know."

Pollyanna paused for breath, and Nancy stammered, "Well—I'm sure it'll be all right."

"I'm *glad* you feel that way. I do, too," nodded Pollyanna, again with a choking little breath. "Of course, 'twould have been a good deal harder to be glad in black—"

"Glad?" gasped Nancy.

"Yes—that Father's gone to Heaven to be with Mother. He said I *must* be glad. It's been pretty hard to do it, even in red gingham. But now it'll be easier because I've got you, Aunt Polly. I'm so glad I've got you!"

"Oh, but you've made an awful mistake, d-dear," Nancy said. "I'm only Nancy. I ain't your Aunt Polly, at all!"

"You—you *aren't*?" said the little girl in dismay.

"I'm Nancy, the hired girl. I do all the work except the washin' an' hard ironin'."

"But there *is* an Aunt Polly?" demanded the child anxiously. "You know she's all the aunt I've got. Father told me she lived in a lovely, great big house way on top of a hill."

"She does. You can see it now, you can," said Nancy. "It's that big white one with the green blinds, way ahead."

CHAPTER TWO

The Little Attic Room

Miss Polly Harrington looked up from her book as Nancy and the little girl appeared in the doorway. Miss Polly coldly held out a hand.

"How do you do, Pollyanna? I—" She had no chance to say more. Pollyanna had flown across the room and flung herself into her aunt's lap.

"Oh, Aunt Polly, Aunt Polly, I don't know how to be glad enough that you let me come to live with you," she was sobbing. "You don't know how perfectly lovely it is to have you and Nancy and all this after I've had just the Ladies' Aid!"

"Yes, well," said Miss Polly, trying to unclasp the girl. "You had a trunk, I presume?"

"Oh, yes, indeed, Aunt Polly. I've got a beautiful trunk that the Ladies' Aid gave me. I haven't got much in it—of my own, I mean. There were all Father's books. You see, Father—"

"Pollyanna," interrupted her aunt sharply, "there is one thing you should understand right away. I do not wish to have you talking about your father to me."

The little girl drew in her breath timidly.

"We will go upstairs to your room. You may follow me, Pollyanna."

Pollyanna turned quietly and followed her aunt from the room. Her eyes were brimming with tears, but her chin was bravely high.

"After all, I reckon I'm glad she doesn't want me to talk about Father," Pollyanna thought. "It'll be easier, maybe, if I don't talk about him. Probably that is why she told me not to—out of—kindness to me." And Pollyanna blinked off the tears and looked happily about her.

Pollyanna's small feet pattered behind her aunt. Her big blue eyes took in all the beautiful furniture, carpets, and pictures. She didn't want to miss anything in this wonderful house. Which door led to the room that was to be her very own?

Would it be beautiful and full of lace curtains, rugs, and pictures? Her aunt opened a door… but it only led to another stairway—a dreary stairway with bare walls on either side. At the top of the stairs were low, shadowy halls and corners stacked with trunks and boxes. Then she saw that her aunt had thrown open a door at the right.

"Pollyanna, here is your room, and your trunk is here, I see. Do you have your trunk key?"

Pollyanna nodded. Her eyes were a little wide and frightened.

Her aunt frowned.

"When I ask a question, Pollyanna, I prefer that you answer aloud, not merely with your head."

"Yes, Aunt Polly."

"Thank you. That is better. I believe you have everything that you need here," she added. "I will send Nancy up to help you unpack. Supper is at six o'clock." She left the room briskly.

For a moment Pollyanna stood quite still, looking after her. Then she turned her wide eyes to the bare wall, the bare floor, the bare windows. She turned them last to the little trunk and stumbled blindly toward it. She fell on her knees at its side, covering her face with her hands.

Nancy found her there when she came up a few minutes later.

"There, there, you poor lamb," Nancy crooned, hugging the little girl. "I was just a-fearin' I'd find you like this. Come, we'll get inside this trunk and take out your dresses in no time."

Nancy's quick hands unpacked the books, the patched underclothes, and the few pitiful dresses. Pollyanna, smiling bravely now, flew about, hanging the dresses in the closet. She stacked the books on the table and put away the underclothes in the dresser drawers.

"I'm sure it's going to be a very nice room. Don't you think so?" the girl stammered, after a while. "And I can be glad there isn't any looking glass here, for then I can't see my freckles."

At one of the windows, Pollyanna gave a glad cry and clapped her hands joyously.

"Oh, Nancy, I hadn't seen this before," she breathed. "Look 'way off there, with those trees and the houses and that lovely church spire, and the river shining just like silver. Why, Nancy, nobody needs any pictures on the wall with *that* to look at. Oh, I'm so *glad* now she let me have this room!"

"If you ain't a little angel from Heaven," cried Nancy. "Oh, land! There's her bell!" Nancy sprang to her feet and dashed out of the room.

Left alone, Pollyanna went back to her "picture." After a time she touched the window sash slowly… It was *so* hot in the room… To her joy the sash moved, and the next moment the window was wide open! Pollyanna leaned far out, drinking in the fresh, sweet air. A huge tree flung its branches against the window, like outstretched arms, inviting her. Suddenly she laughed aloud.

The next moment she had climbed to the window ledge. From there it was easy to step to the nearest tree branch. Clinging like a monkey, she swung herself from limb to limb until she reached the lowest branch. The drop to the ground was a little fearsome, but she landed on all fours, picked herself up, and looked eagerly about.

She was at the back of the house. Before her lay a garden where a bent old man was working. Beyond the garden a little path led up a steep hill. At the top, a lone pine tree stood beside a huge rock. To Pollyanna, at the moment, there seemed to be just one place in the world worth being—the top of that big rock.

With a run, Pollyanna skipped by the bent old man, and made her way between the rows of green growing things. A little out of breath, she reached the path, then began to climb. Already, however, she was thinking what a long way off that rock must be. Back at the window it had looked so near!

Fifteen minutes later the great clock in the hallway of the Harrington home struck six. At the last stroke Nancy sounded the bell for supper.

One, two, three minutes passed. Miss Polly frowned and tapped the floor with her shoe. She rose to her feet, went into the hall, and looked upstairs. She listened for a minute, then turned and swept into the dining room.

"Nancy," she said, as soon as the serving-maid appeared, "my niece is late. You need not call her. I told her what time supper was, and now she will have to suffer the consequences. When she comes down she may have bread and milk in the kitchen."

After supper, Nancy crept up the back stairs to the attic room.

"Bread and milk, indeed, when the poor lamb has only just cried herself to sleep," she muttered. She softly pushed open the door. The next moment she gave a frightened cry. "Where are you? Where've you gone? Where *have* you gone?" she panted. She looked in the closet, under the bed, and even in the trunk and down the water pitcher. Then she flew downstairs and out to Old Tom, the gardener.

"Mr. Tom, Mr. Tom, that blessed child's gone," she wailed. "She's vanished right up into Heaven where she come from, poor lamb!"

The old man straightened up.

"Gone? Heaven? Well, Nancy, it do look like as if she'd tried to get to Heaven," he agreed. He pointed with a crooked finger to where a slender figure was poised on top of a huge rock.

CHAPTER THREE

The Game

"For land's sake, Miss Pollyanna, what a scare you did give me," panted Nancy. She hurried up to the big rock as Pollyanna slid down.

"I didn't even know you'd went," cried Nancy, tucking the little girl's hand under her arm and hurrying her down the hill. "Poor little lamb! And you must be hungry, too. I'm afraid you'll have to have bread and milk in the kitchen with me, because you didn't come down to supper."

"But I couldn't. I was up here."

"Yes, but—she didn't know that, you see!" chuckled Nancy. "I'm sorry about the bread and milk, I am, I am."

"Oh, I'm not. I'm glad."

"Glad? Why?"

"Why, I like bread and milk, and I'd like to eat with you. I don't see any trouble about being glad about that."

"You don't seem to see any trouble bein' glad about everythin'," replied Nancy.

Pollyanna laughed softly. "Well, that's the game, you know, anyway."

"The—*game*?"

"Yes, the 'just being glad' game. Father told it to me, and it's lovely," said Pollyanna. "We've played it always, ever since I was a little, little girl. We began it when some crutches came in a missionary barrel."

"*Crutches!*"

"Yes. You see, I'd wanted a doll. But when the barrel came the lady wrote that no dolls came in, just the little crutches. So she sent 'em along. The game was to find something about everything to be glad about, no matter what," said Pollyanna. "We began right then—on the crutches."

"Well, goodness me! I can't see anythin' to be glad about—gettin' a pair of crutches when you wanted a doll."

"There is—there is," Pollyanna crowed. "*I* couldn't see it, either, Nancy, at first. Father had to tell it to me. You just be glad because you *don't—need—'em!* You see, it's easy when you know how! Only sometimes it's almost too hard, like when your father goes to Heaven."

"Yes, or when you're put in a snippy little room 'way at the top of the house with nothin' in it," growled Nancy.

Pollyanna sighed. "That was a hard one, at first, 'specially when I was so lonesome and I *had* been wanting pretty things! Then I saw that lovely picture out the window, so I knew I'd found things to be glad about. You see, when you're hunting for the glad things, you sort of forget the other kind. I suppose, though, it'll be a little harder now, since I haven't anybody to play the game with..." Then she added brightly, "Maybe Aunt Polly will play it, though!"

"My stars and stockings!—*Her?*" Nancy said to herself. Aloud she said, "Pollyanna, I ain't sayin' that I'll play it very well, but I'll play the game with ye, somehow—I just will, I will!"

"Oh, Nancy," cried Pollyanna, giving her a hug. "That'll be splendid! We'll have such fun!"

Pollyanna ate her bread and milk cheerfully. Then she went into the sitting room, where her aunt sat reading. Miss Polly looked up coldly.

"Have you had your supper, Pollyanna?"

"Yes, Aunt Polly."

"I'm very sorry, Pollyanna, that I had to send you into the kitchen to eat bread and milk."

"But I was real glad you did it, Aunt Polly. I like bread and milk, and Nancy, too. You mustn't feel bad about that one bit."

Aunt Polly sat suddenly a little more straight in her chair.

"Pollyanna, it's quite time you were in bed. You have had a hard day. Tomorrow we must plan your hours and see what new clothes you might need. Nancy will give you a candle. Breakfast will be at half-past seven. See that you are on time. Good night."

Pollyanna came straight to her aunt's side and gave her a loving hug. "I've had such a beautiful time, so far," she sighed happily. "I know I'm going to just love living with you. Good night," she called cheerfully, as she ran from the room.

"Well, upon my soul!" exclaimed Miss Polly. "What an extraordinary child."

Fifteen minutes later, in the attic room, a lonely little girl sobbed into the tightly-clutched sheet.

"I know, Father-among-the-angels, I'm not playing the game one bit now—not one bit. But I don't believe even you could find anything to be glad about sleeping all alone 'way off up here in the dark—like this. If only I was near Nancy or even Aunt Polly, it would be easier!"

It was nearly seven o'clock when Pollyanna awoke the next day. The air blew in fresh and sweet. The birds were twittering joyously, and Pollyanna flew to the window to talk to them. There, below her window, was Aunt Polly among the rosebushes. Pollyanna quickly dressed and sped down the stairs, leaving both doors open.

"Oh, Aunt Polly!" she called out. "I reckon I am glad this morning just to be alive!"

But Aunt Polly was not glad when she found flies buzzing about at breakfast. Nor was she glad that they had come in through the attic windows! Heat or no heat, the windows were to be shut!

Pollyanna's patched and worn-out clothes were also a disappointment.

"Pollyanna, we will drive to town at half-past one this afternoon," Aunt Polly said. "Not one of these things is fit for my niece to wear. You'll enter school in the fall. Meanwhile, I wish to hear you read aloud half an hour each day."

"I love to read," cried the girl. "I like to read to myself, on account of the big words, you know."

"It is also my duty to see that you are properly instructed in music," went on Aunt Polly. "I shall teach you sewing myself, of course. And you shall learn how to cook…" She paused, then went on slowly. "At nine o'clock every morning you will read aloud to me. Before that you will put this room in order. Wednesday and Saturday after half-past nine, you will spend with Nancy in the kitchen, learning to cook. Other mornings you will sew with me. That leaves afternoons for your music," she finished, and arose from her chair.

Pollyanna cried out in dismay, "Oh, but Aunt Polly, Aunt Polly, you haven't left me any time at all just to live! I'd be *breathing* all the time I was doing those things, but I wouldn't be living. Playing outdoors, reading, climbing hills, talking to Nancy. That's what I call living, Aunt Polly."

"Pollyanna! You will be allowed a proper amount of playtime, of course. But if I am willing to see that you have proper care and instruction, *you* must see that they are not wasted."

"Oh, Aunt Polly, as if I ever could be ungrateful. Why, *I love you!*"

"Yes, well, I *will* do my duty by you," said Miss Polly. She turned toward the door.

Indeed, Miss Polly *did* do her duty by her in many respects. She did take her to town for new church dresses and school clothes. She did sign her up for school in the fall. She fed her promptly three times a day, and allowed for playtime.

What Miss Polly did *not* offer—what her heart could not offer—Pollyanna found in other ways. With Nancy she played the "glad game," and talked about her father. With the family gardener, Old Tom, she talked of her mother. He would sit and tell her all he remembered about "Miss Jennie." And in the birds and the flowers and the outdoors, she found comfort.

When Miss Polly found the little girl sleeping out under the stars on the flat roof of the sunroom, she *finally* did her duty and moved her out of the hot attic room. Pollyanna was moved to the room below—and she was delighted to find it also had a lovely "picture window."

CHAPTER FOUR

Pollyanna Goes Visiting

It was not long before life at the Harrington home settled into order. Pollyanna sewed, practiced music, read aloud, and studied cooking, it is true. But she did not spend as much time on these as her aunt had planned.

She had more time to "just live." Almost every afternoon from two until six o'clock was hers to do with as she liked. There were no children in the neighborhood for Pollyanna to play with. The house itself was on the outskirts of the village. But she told Nancy, "I'm happy just to walk around and see the streets and the houses and watch the people. I just love people. Don't you?"

Almost every pleasant afternoon Pollyanna begged for an errand to run, so that she might be off for a walk. It was on these walks that she often met "the Man." The Man wore a long black coat and a high silk hat. His face was clean-shaven and rather pale and his hair was somewhat gray. He walked stiffly, and rather rapidly, and he was always alone. Pollyanna felt a little sorry for him. Perhaps that is why she spoke to him one day.

"How do you do, sir? Isn't this a nice day?" she called cheerily as she approached him.

The man stopped uncertainly.

"Did you speak—to me?" he asked sharply.

"Yes, sir," she beamed. "It's a nice day, isn't it?"

"Eh? Oh! Humph!" he grunted, and strode off.

Pollyanna laughed. He was such a funny man. The next day she saw him again.

"It isn't quite so nice as yesterday, but it's pretty nice," she called out cheerfully.

"Eh? Oh! Humph!" grunted the man, and once again Pollyanna laughed.

When for the third time Pollyanna talked to him, the man stopped.

"See here, child, who are you, and why are you speaking to me every day?"

"I'm Pollyanna Whittier, and I thought you looked lonesome. I'm so glad you stopped. Now we've met—only I don't know your name yet."

"Well, of all the—" The man did not finish his sentence, but strode on faster than ever.

Pollyanna looked after him. "But that was only half an introduction. I don't know *his* name, yet," she murmured, and went on her way.

Pollyanna was carrying calf's-foot jelly to Mrs. Snow today. Miss Polly sent something to Mrs. Snow once a week, since Mrs. Snow was poor, sick, and a member of her church. Today Pollyanna had begged to go, and Miss Polly had allowed it.

Pollyanna knocked on the door of the shabby little cottage. A pale, tired-looking girl answered.

"How do you do?" began Pollyanna politely. "I'm from Miss Polly Harrington, and I'd like to see Mrs. Snow, please."

"I'm Milly, her daughter. Please follow me."

In the sickroom, Pollyanna blinked a little in the gloom. Then she saw a woman half-sitting up in the bed across the room.

"How do you do, Mrs. Snow? Aunt Polly says she hopes you are comfortable today. She's sent you some calf's-foot jelly."

"Dear me," said a fretful voice. "And I was hoping for lamb broth today."

The sick woman pulled herself up till she sat up in the bed. It was a most unusual thing for her to do, though Pollyanna did not know this.

"I'm Pollyanna Whittier. I'm Miss Polly Harrington's niece, and I've come to live with her. That's why I'm here this morning."

"Very well, thank you. Your aunt is very kind, of course. But my appetite isn't very good this morning." She stopped suddenly, then went on, "I never slept a wink last night—not a wink!"

"Oh, dear, I wish *I* didn't," sighed Pollyanna. "You lose such a lot of time just sleeping! Don't you think so?"

"Lose time—sleeping?" exclaimed the woman.

"Yes, when you might be just living, you know. It seems such a pity we can't live nights, too."

The woman pulled herself higher up in bed.

"Well, if you ain't an amazing young one!" she cried. "Go to that window and pull up the curtain. I would like to know what you look like!"

"Oh, dear! Then you'll see my freckles, won't you?" Pollyanna sighed and went to the window. "There!" she said, as she turned back to the bed. "I'm so glad you wanted to see me, for now I can see you! They didn't tell me you were so pretty!"

"Me!—pretty?" scoffed the woman.

"Your eyes are so big and dark, and your hair's dark, too, and curly," cooed Pollyanna. "Why, Mrs. Snow, you *are* pretty! Just let me show you!"

Pollyanna skipped over to the dresser and picked up a small mirror.

"If you don't mind, I'd like to fix your hair just a little before I let you see it. May I, please?"

For five minutes Pollyanna worked swiftly. Meanwhile, the sick woman was beginning to feel excited in spite of herself.

"There!" panted Pollyanna, plucking a pink flower from a vase nearby and tucking it into the dark hair. She held out the mirror.

"Humph!" grunted the sick woman, eyeing her reflection. "I like red flowers better than pink ones. But then they fade anyhow before night, so what's the difference?"

"But you should be glad they fade! Then you can get more! And then I could fix your hair again. I love your black hair. It shows up so much nicer on a pillow than yellow hair does! I would be so glad if I only had it," sighed Pollyanna.

Mrs. Snow let the mirror drop.

"Well, you wouldn't if you were me. You wouldn't be glad for black hair nor anything else, if you had to lie here all day as I do!"

Pollyanna frowned. "It would be kind of hard to be glad about things, wouldn't it?" she said.

"Be glad about things—when you're sick in bed? I should say it would," replied Mrs. Snow.

"Tell me something to be glad about!"

To Mrs. Snow's amazement, Pollyanna sprang to her feet and clapped her hands.

"Oh, goody! That'll be a hard one—won't it? I've got to go, now, but I'll think and think all the way home. Good-bye. I've had a lovely time!" she called, as she tripped through the doorway.

"Well, I never! Now, what does she mean by that?" exclaimed Mrs. Snow, staring after her.

It rained the next time Pollyanna saw the Man. She greeted him, however, with a bright smile.

"It isn't so nice today, is it?" she called gleefully. "I'm glad it doesn't rain always!"

The Man stopped, with a scowl on his face.

"See here, little girl, we might just as well settle this once and for all. I've got something besides the weather to think of. I don't know whether the sun shines or not."

Pollyanna smiled. "No, sir, I thought you didn't. That's why I told you, so you would notice that the sun shines. I knew you'd be glad it did if you stopped to think of it!"

"Well, of all the—" he exclaimed, as he turned and strode on as before.

The next time Pollyanna met the Man, his eyes were gazing straight into hers.

"Good afternoon," he greeted her a little stiffly. "I *know* the sun is shining today."

The Man always spoke to Pollyanna after this, though usually he said just "Good afternoon." Even that, however, was a great surprise to Nancy, who was with Pollyanna one day when he passed.

"Sakes alive, Miss Pollyanna," she gasped, "did that man *speak to you*? Do you know who he is?"

Pollyanna frowned and shook her head.

"He hasn't spoken to anybody for years, child, except when he just has to. He's John Pendleton. He lives by himself in the big house on Pendleton Hill. He's got loads of money. Nobody in town is as rich as he is. But he ain't spending his money. He's a-savin' it."

"Oh, for the poor people," Pollyanna decided. "How perfectly splendid!"

Several days later, Pollyanna went to see Mrs. Snow and found her again in a darkened room.

"Oh, it's you, is it?" asked a fretful voice from the bed. "I wish you had come yesterday. I *wanted* you yesterday."

"Did you? Well, I'm glad 'tisn't any farther away from yesterday than today is, then," laughed Pollyanna. She came cheerily into the room and set her basket carefully down on a chair. "How do you do today?"

"Very poorly, thank you," murmured Mrs. Snow. "I haven't been able to nap all day."

Polly nodded sympathetically.

"I almost forgot—but I've thought it up, Mrs. Snow—what you can be glad about."

"*Glad* about! What do you mean?"

"Why, don't you remember? You asked me to tell you something to be glad about—even though you did have to lie here in bed all day."

"Oh!" scoffed the woman. "*That?* Yes, I remember that. But I didn't suppose you were serious about it."

"Oh, yes, I was," nodded Pollyanna, "and I found it, too."

"Did you, really? Well, what is it?"

Pollyanna drew a long breath.

"I thought how glad you could be that other folks weren't like you—all sick in bed like this, you know," she announced.

Mrs. Snow stared. Her eyes were angry.

"Well, really!" she exclaimed.

"And now I'll tell you the game," said Pollyanna cheerfully. And she began to tell of the missionary barrel, the crutches, and the doll that did not come.

The story was just finished when Milly appeared at the door.

"Your aunt is wanting you, Miss Pollyanna. She says you're to hurry—that you've got some practicing to make up before dark."

Pollyanna rose reluctantly.

"All right," she sighed. "I'll hurry." Suddenly she laughed. "I suppose I ought to be glad I've got legs to hurry with, hadn't I, Mrs. Snow? Good-bye!"

There was no answer. Mrs. Snow's eyes were closed. But Milly, whose eyes were wide open with surprise, saw that there were tears on the pale, thin cheeks.

CHAPTER FIVE

Pollyanna to the Rescue

August came. August brought several surprises and some changes—none of which really surprised Nancy. Ever since Pollyanna's arrival, Nancy had looked for surprises and changes.

First there was the kitten Pollyanna found mewing down the road and brought home.

"And I was glad I didn't find anyone who owned it," she told her aunt happily. "I love kitties. I knew you'd be glad to let it live here."

Miss Polly opened her lips and tried to speak—but she could think of nothing to say. She was held fast by the same helpless feeling that had been hers so often since Pollyanna's arrival.

The next day it was a dog, even dirtier and sadder, perhaps, than the kitten. Again Miss Polly found herself as the kind protector and angel of mercy. And she was a woman who disliked dogs even more than cats, if possible!

However, when, in less than a week, Pollyanna brought home a small, ragged boy, Miss Polly *did* have something to say.

On a pleasant Thursday morning, Pollyanna had been taking food again to Mrs. Snow. Mrs. Snow and Pollyanna were the best of friends now, and she and Mrs. Snow were playing the "glad game" together. Mrs. Snow had been sorry for everything for so long that it was not easy to be glad for anything now. But under Pollyanna's cheery instruction and merry laughter at her mistakes, she was learning fast.

Pollyanna was thinking of this now when suddenly she saw the boy, sitting in a hopeless little heap by the roadside, whittling half-heartedly at a small stick.

"Hullo," smiled Pollyanna.

The boy glanced up, but he looked away again, at once.

"Hullo yourself," he mumbled.

Pollyanna hesitated, then dropped herself comfortably down on the grass near him.

"My name's Pollyanna Whittier," she began pleasantly. "What's yours?"

The boy stirred restlessly. He even almost got to his feet. But he settled back.

"Jimmy Bean," he grunted.

"Good! Now we're introduced. I live at Miss Polly Harrington's house. Where do you live?"

"Nowhere."

"Nowhere! Why, everybody lives somewhere," said Pollyanna.

"Well, I don't—just now. I'm a-huntin' up a new place."

"Oh! Where is it?"

"Silly! I wouldn't be huntin' if I knew!"

Pollyanna tossed her head. This was not a nice boy, and she did not like to be called "silly." Still, he was somebody besides old folks. "Where did you live before?" she asked.

The boy gave a short laugh, but his face looked a little pleasanter when he spoke this time.

"I'm Jimmy Bean, and I'm ten years old goin' on eleven. I come last year to live at the Orphans' Home. They've got so many kids, though, there ain't much room for me. I'd *like* a home. If ye has a home, ye has folks, an' I ain't had folks since my dad died. I've tried four houses, but they didn't want me."

"Oh, dear! I know just how you feel," said Pollyanna. "After my father died there wasn't anybody for me till Aunt Polly said she'd take—" Pollyanna stopped. She had a wonderful idea.

"Oh, I know just the place for you," she cried. "Aunt Polly'll take you—I know she will! Didn't she take me? And didn't she take Fluffy and Buffy? And they're only cats and dogs. You don't know how good and kind she is!"

Pollyanna quickly led her companion straight into the presence of her amazed aunt.

"Oh, Aunt Polly," she beamed, "just look here! I've got something ever so much nicer than Fluffy and Buffy for you to bring up. It's a real live boy. He won't mind a bit sleeping in the attic and he says he'll work."

Miss Polly grew white, then very red.

"Pollyanna, who is this dirty little boy? Where did you find him?" she demanded sharply.

The "dirty little boy" fell back a step and looked toward the door. Pollyanna laughed merrily.

"There, I forgot to tell you his name! This is Jimmy Bean, Aunt Polly."

"Well, what is he doing here?"

"Why, Aunt Polly, I just told you! He's for you. I brought him home so he could live here. I told him how good you were to me, and to Fluffy and Buffy. I knew you would be to him, because of course he's even nicer than cats and dogs…"

"That will *do*, Pollyanna! This is the most absurd thing you've done yet. As if tramp cats and mangy dogs weren't bad enough, you must bring home ragged little beggars from the street!"

The boy's eyes flashed and his chin came up. "I ain't a beggar, ma'am!" he stormed. With two strides of his sturdy little legs he left the room.

"Oh, Aunt Polly," choked Pollyanna. "Why, I thought you'd be *glad* to have him here! Oh!" She broke off, hurrying blindly from the room.

Before the boy had reached the end of the driveway, Pollyanna caught up to him.

"Boy! Boy! Jimmy Bean, I want you to know how sorry I am," she panted.

"Sorry nothin'! I ain't blamin' you," replied the boy. "But I ain't no beggar."

"Of course you aren't! But you mustn't blame Auntie," appealed Pollyanna. "She is good and kind. I probably didn't explain it right. I do wish I could find some place for you, though!"

The little boy shrugged his shoulders and turned away.

Pollyanna did not turn her steps toward home. She was sure that nothing would do her quite as much good as a walk through the green quiet of Pendleton Woods. Suddenly Pollyanna lifted her head and listened. A dog had barked some distance ahead. A moment later he came dashing toward her, still barking.

"Hullo, doggie—hullo!" Pollyanna snapped her fingers at the dog and looked down the path. She had seen the dog once before, with the Man, Mr. John Pendleton. For some minutes she watched eagerly, but he did not appear. Then she turned her attention toward the dog.

He was acting strangely, giving short, sharp yelps of alarm, running back and forth in the path ahead. At last Pollyanna understood, turned, and followed him.

It was not long before Pollyanna came upon the reason for it all. A man was lying motionless at the foot of a steep, overhanging rock a few yards from the path. With a cry of dismay Pollyanna ran to his side.

"Mr. Pendleton! Oh, are you hurt?"

"Hurt? Oh, no! I'm just taking a nap in the sunshine," snapped the Man. "There, there, child, I beg your pardon. It's only this confounded leg of mine." He paused, and with some difficulty reached into a pocket and then handed her a key.

"Now, listen. Straight through the path, about five minutes' walk, is my house. On the big desk you'll find a telephone. Call Dr. Thomas Chilton and tell him that John Pendleton is at the foot of Little Eagle Ledge with a broken leg. He'll know what to do."

With a little sobbing cry, Pollyanna went. It was not long before she came in sight of the gray stone mansion. She sped across the untidy lawn and around to the side door. Her fingers were stiff from clutching the keys so tightly, but at last the heavy, carved door swung slowly open.

Pollyanna ran through the hall to the door at the end and opened it. The room was large, dark and somber. Through the west window the sun's rays shone gold across the floor and the tarnished brass of the fireplace. The walls were lined with books. The floor was littered with paper. Everywhere was dust, dust, dust. In the middle of the room was the large desk with the telephone.

In due time she had Dr. Chilton himself at the other end of the phone. She fearfully delivered her message and answered the doctor's short, direct questions. This done, she hung up the receiver and drew a long breath of relief.

In what seemed, even to the injured man, an incredibly short time, Pollyanna was back in the woods at the man's side.

"The doctor will be right up just as soon as possible with the men and things," she said. "He knew just where you were, so I came back here. I wanted to be with you to hold your head."

"You are so kind, even though I'm…" said the Man, wincing with pain.

"Even though you're so—cross?" said the girl.

"Thanks for your honesty. Yes."

Pollyanna laughed. "But you're only cross on the *outside*. You aren't cross on the inside one bit. I can tell by the way this dog loves you."

Minutes passed and the sky darkened. At last the dog perked up his ears and gave a short, sharp bark. Pollyanna heard voices, and very soon three men appeared with a stretcher. The tallest was a smooth-shaven, kind-eyed man whom Pollyanna knew by sight as "Dr. Chilton."

"Well, my little lady, playing nurse?" the doctor asked cheerily.

"Oh, no, sir," smiled Pollyanna. "I've only held his head. But I'm glad I was here."

"So am I," nodded Dr. Chilton, as he turned his attention to the injured man.

Pollyanna was a little late for supper on the night of the accident to John Pendleton, but as it happened she escaped without punishment.

Nancy met her at the door and explained that Aunt Polly had been called out of town for a few days to attend a funeral.

Then, with an open mouth and wide eyes, Nancy listened to Pollyanna tell of the accident—and about her being inside that big, dreary, gray stone house!

CHAPTER SIX

Just a Matter of Jelly

It was about a week after the accident in Pendleton Woods that Pollyanna said to her aunt one morning, "Aunt Polly, please would you mind if I took Mrs. Snow's calf's-foot jelly this week to someone else? You let me take jelly to *her*, so I thought you would to *him*—this once. His broken leg won't last forever, and she can have all the rest of the things after just once or twice."

"He? Broken leg? What are you talking about, Pollyanna?"

Pollyanna stared. Then her face relaxed.

"Oh, I forgot you didn't know. I found him in the woods, and I had to unlock his house and

telephone for the men and the doctor, and hold his head, and everything. And then I came away and haven't seen him since. So I thought how nice it would be if I could take the calf's-foot jelly to him just this once. Aunt Polly, may I?"

"Yes, yes, I suppose so," agreed Miss Polly. "Who did you say he was?"

"The Man. I mean, Mr. John Pendleton."

Miss Polly almost sprang from her chair.

"*John Pendleton!*"

"Yes. Nancy told me his name. Maybe you know him."

Miss Polly did not answer. Instead she asked, "Do *you* know him?"

"Oh, yes. He always speaks and smiles—now. I'll go and get the jelly," finished Pollyanna, already halfway across the room.

"Pollyanna, wait!" Miss Polly's voice was suddenly very stern. "I've changed my mind. I would prefer that Mrs. Snow had that jelly today. I do not care to send it to John Pendleton."

Pollyanna's face fell. "I know, he is cross—outside," she admitted sadly, "and I suppose you don't like him. But I wouldn't say 'twas you who sent it. I'd say 'twas me."

Miss Polly began to shake her head again. Then, suddenly, she stopped, and asked quietly, "Does he know who you are, Pollyanna? Does he know you are my niece?"

The little girl sighed. "I reckon not."

Miss Polly was looking at Pollyanna with eyes that did not seem to see her at all. Then she pulled herself up stiffly.

"Very well, Pollyanna," she said at last. "You may take the jelly to Mr. Pendleton as your gift. But be very sure that he does not think I sent it!"

"Thank you, Aunt Polly," exulted Pollyanna, as she flew through the door.

John Pendleton's great house looked very different to Pollyanna when she made her second visit. Windows were open. An elderly woman was hanging out clothes in the back yard. The doctor's carriage stood near the door.

A familiar small dog bounded up the steps to greet her. After a slight delay the woman who had been hanging out the clothes opened the door.

"If you please, I've brought some calf's-foot jelly for Mr. Pendleton," smiled Pollyanna.

The doctor, coming into the hall, stepped quickly forward.

"Ah! Some calf's-foot jelly?" he asked. "Fine! Maybe you'd like to see our patient, eh?"

"Oh, yes, sir," beamed Pollyanna, and a few moments later found herself alone with a very cross-looking man lying flat on his back in bed.

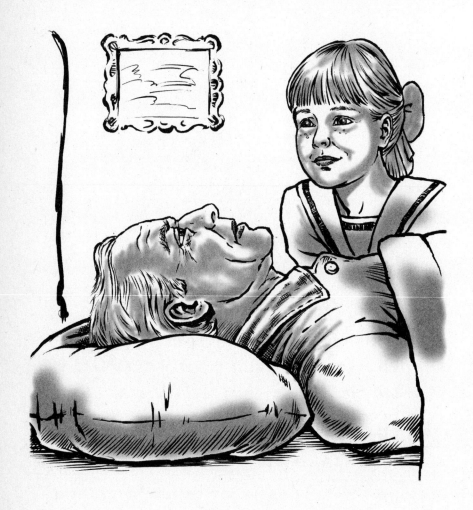

"See here, didn't I say—" began an angry voice. "Oh, it's you!" it broke off, as Pollyanna walked toward the bed. In spite of himself the man smiled, but all he said was "Humph!"

"I've brought you some jelly," said Pollyanna. "I hope you like it."

"Yes, yes, well. I'm flat on my back right here this minute, and I'll probably stay here till doomsday, I guess."

Pollyanna looked shocked.

"Oh, no! Broken legs don't last, and you didn't break but one. You can be glad 'twasn't two."

"Of course! So fortunate," sniffed the man, with uplifted eyebrows. "I suppose I might be glad I wasn't a centipede and didn't break fifty!"

Pollyanna chuckled and sat on the bed.

"Oh, of course," the man went on, "I can be glad, too, for all the rest, I suppose—the nurse, and the doctor, and that woman in the kitchen!"

"Why, yes, sir! Think how bad 'twould be if you *didn't* have them—you lying here like this!"

"You expect me to be glad for a woman who rearranges my house? And a man who aids her, and calls it 'nursing'? And a doctor who eggs 'em on? And they all expect me to pay them for it!"

Pollyanna frowned sympathetically.

"Yes, I know. *That* part is too bad—about the money—when you've been saving it all this time."

"Child, what are you talking about?"

Pollyanna smiled radiantly.

"About your money, you know, and saving it for the poor. You see, I found out about it. Nancy told me."

The man's jaw dropped.

"Well, may I inquire who Nancy is?"

"Our Nancy. She works for Aunt Polly, Polly Harrington. I live with her."

The man made a sudden movement.

"Miss—Polly—Harrington!" he breathed. "You live with *her*?"

"Yes. She's taken me to bring up on account of my mother, you know," faltered Pollyanna. "She's my mother's sister. After Father went to be with Mother in Heaven, there wasn't anyone left for me. So Aunt Polly took me."

The man did not answer. His face was so white that Pollyanna was frightened. She rose timidly to her feet

"I reckon maybe I'd better go now," she said quietly. "I hope you'll like the jelly."

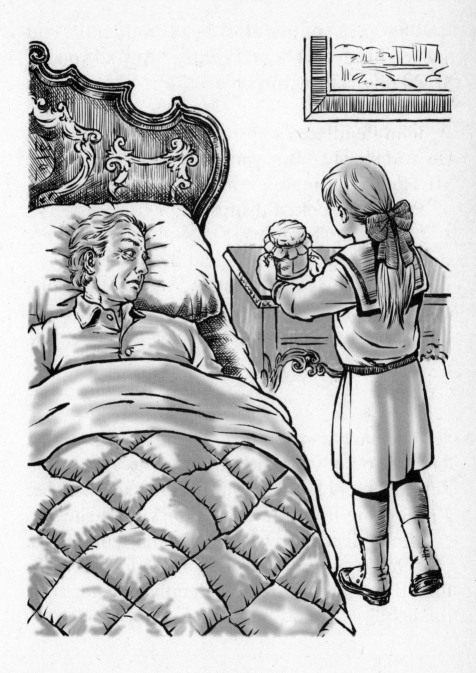

The man turned his head suddenly, and opened his eyes. He said gently, "And so you are Miss Polly Harrington's niece?"

"Yes, sir."

John Pendleton's lips curved in an odd smile. He said slowly, "But you can't mean that it was Miss Polly Harrington who sent that jelly to me?"

Pollyanna looked distressed.

"N-no, sir, she didn't. She said I must be very sure not to let you think she did send it."

"I thought as much," stated the man, turning away his head. And Pollyanna, still more distressed, tiptoed from the room.

Pollyanna was not the only one distressed that day. Aunt Polly seemed quite distressed when Pollyanna told her that Dr. Chilton had given her a ride home from Mr. Pendleton's. And she was even *more* distressed when Pollyanna announced:

"Don't worry, Aunt Polly. I told Mr. Pendleton that *you* most certainly did not send the jelly!"

CHAPTER SEVEN

A Red Rose and a Lace Shawl

One rainy day, Miss Polly went to a meeting of the Ladies' Aid Society. When she returned, her cheeks were a bright, pretty pink, and her hair, blown by the damp wind, had fluffed into curls. Pollyanna had never seen her aunt look like this.

"Oh—oh! Why, Aunt Polly, you've got 'em, too," she cried joyfully, dancing around her aunt.

"Got what, you impossible child?"

"No, no, please, Aunt Polly! Don't smooth 'em out! Those darling little black curls. Oh, please, may I do your hair like I did Mrs. Snow's, and put in a flower? Why, you'd be ever so much prettier! You *will* let me do your hair, won't you?"

"Pollyanna!" Miss Polly spoke very sharply. Yet, Pollyanna's words had given her an odd feeling of joy. When before had anybody cared how she, or her hair, looked? When before had anybody "loved" to see her "pretty"?

"You didn't say I *couldn't* do your hair," Pollyanna crowed. "Now wait just where you are. I'll get a comb."

"But, Pollyanna, I—I—" But to her amazement, Miss Polly found herself in a chair with Pollyanna eagerly primping and fussing over her.

"Oh, my! what pretty hair you've got," chattered Pollyanna, "and there's so much more of it than Mrs. Snow has, too! Why, Aunt Polly, I'll make you so pretty everybody'll just love to look at you!"

"Pollyanna!" gasped a voice from a veil of hair. "I—I'm sure I don't know why I'm letting you do this silly thing."

"But, Aunt Polly—don't you like to look at pretty things? Now don't peek—I'll be right back!"

But, of course, Miss Polly *did* peek. She caught a glimpse of herself in the mirror of the dressing table. What she saw sent a flush of rosy color to her cheeks.

She saw a face—not young, it is true—but alight with excitement and surprise. The cheeks were a pretty pink. The eyes sparkled. The dark hair lay in loose waves about the forehead. It curved back over the ears, with softening little curls here and there.

Pollyanna rushed back in with a beautiful shawl, yellowed from being packed away, and scented with lavender. With trembling fingers, Pollyanna draped it about her aunt's shoulders. One touch was still needed. She pulled her aunt toward the sun parlor where she could see a red rose blooming within reach of her hand.

"Only a minute! I'll have you ready now quicker'n no time," panted Pollyanna, reaching for the rose and thrusting it into the soft hair above Miss Polly's ear. "There!"

For one dazed moment Miss Polly looked at herself. Then, something out the open windows of the sun parlor made her give a low cry and flee to her room. It was Dr. Chilton's horse and carriage turning into the driveway.

Delightedly, Pollyanna called out, "Dr. Chilton! Did you want to see me? I'm up here."

"Yes!" he said. "Will you come down, please?"

In the bedroom Pollyanna found a flushed-faced, angry-eyed woman plucking at the pins that held a lace shawl in place.

"Pollyanna, how could you?" moaned the woman. "Letting me be seen like this!"

"But you looked lovely, perfectly lovely, Aunt Polly, and—"

The woman flung the shawl to one side and attacked her hair with shaking fingers.

"Oh, dear! And you did look so pretty," sobbed Pollyanna, as she stumbled through the door and sped downstairs to the waiting doctor.

"I've prescribed you for a patient," announced the doctor, "and he's sent me to get the prescription filled. Mr. John Pendleton would like to see you today. Will you come? I'll call for you and bring you back before six o'clock."

"I'd love to! Let me ask Aunt Polly," cried the girl. In a few moments she returned, hat in hand.

"Wasn't it your aunt I saw with you a few minutes ago in the window of the sun parlor?" the doctor asked as they drove away.

Pollyanna drew a long breath.

"Yes, but she's troubled. I dressed her up in a perfectly lovely lace shawl I found upstairs, and

I fixed her hair and put in a rose. She looked so pretty. Didn't *you* think she looked just lovely?"

For a moment the doctor did not answer. When he did speak his voice was so low Pollyanna could barely hear the words.

"Yes, Pollyanna, I thought she did look lovely."

"Did you? I'm so glad! I'll tell her," nodded the little girl.

To her surprise the doctor said, "Pollyanna, I'm afraid I have to ask you not to tell her that."

"Why, Dr. Chilton! Why not? I should think you'd be glad—"

"But she might not be," cut in the doctor.

Pollyanna considered this for a moment.

"Well, maybe she wouldn't," she sighed. "I remember now. It was because she saw you that she ran."

The doctor said nothing. He did not speak again, indeed, until they were almost to the great stone house in which John Pendleton lay with a broken leg.

CHAPTER EIGHT

"A Mystery"

Mr. Pendleton greeted Pollyanna with a smile.

"Well, Miss Pollyanna, I'm thinking you must be a very forgiving little person, or you wouldn't have come to see me today."

"Why, Mr. Pendleton, I was real glad to come, and I'm sure I don't see why I shouldn't be."

"Oh, well, I was pretty cross with you, I'm afraid, the other day when you so kindly brought me the jelly—and that time you found me with the broken leg. I don't think I've ever thanked you."

"But I was glad to find you. That is, I don't mean I was glad your leg was broken, of course," she corrected hurriedly.

John Pendleton smiled.

"I understand and I consider you a very brave little girl to do what you did that day. I thank you for the jelly, too," he added in a lighter voice.

"Did you like it?" asked Pollyanna.

"Very much. I suppose there isn't any more today that Aunt Polly *didn't* send, is there?" he asked with an awkward smile.

"N-no, sir," stammered Pollyanna, blushing. "Please, sir, I didn't mean to be rude the other day when I said Aunt Polly did *not* send the jelly."

"Well, well, this will never do at all! I sent for you so we could have some fun. Listen! Out in the library you will find a carved box in the big case near the fireplace. You may bring it to me. It is heavy, but not too heavy for you to carry."

"Oh, I'm awfully strong," declared Pollyanna cheerfully, as she sprang to her feet. In a minute she had returned with the box.

It was a wonderful half-hour that Pollyanna spent then. The box was full of treasures that John Pendleton had picked up in years of travel. Each had some entertaining story, whether it was carved chessmen from China, or a little jade idol from India.

The visit was delightful. Before it was over, they were talking about Pollyanna's daily life, Nancy, and even Aunt Polly. They were talking, too, of life and home long ago in the faraway Western town.

When it was nearly time for her to go, the man said, in a voice Pollyanna had never before heard from stern John Pendleton:

"I want you to come to see me often. Will you? I'm lonesome, and I need you. There's another reason, too. I thought, after I found out who you were, that I didn't want you to come anymore. You reminded me of something I have tried to forget… But after a time I was wanting to see you so much. Not seeing you was making me remember the thing I wanted to forget. So now I want you to come visit. Will you—little girl?"

Pollyanna's eyes beamed with sympathy for the sad-faced man before her.

"Why, yes, Mr. Pendleton," she said. "I'd love to come visit you!"

After supper that evening, Pollyanna sat with Nancy on the back porch. She told her all about Mr. John Pendleton's wonderful carved box, and the still more wonderful things it contained.

"I don't see why everybody thinks he's so bad, Nancy," Pollyanna said. "They wouldn't, if they knew him. But even Aunt Polly doesn't like him very well."

"What beats me is how he took to you so, Miss Pollyanna," Nancy said. "He ain't the sort o' man what gen'rally takes to kids, he ain't, he ain't."

Pollyanna smiled.

"I reckon he didn't want to *all* the time. Why, only today he said that once he felt he never wanted to see me again, because I reminded him of something he wanted to forget."

"What's that?" interrupted Nancy excitedly. "He said ye reminded him of something he wanted to forget?"

"He didn't tell me what. He just said it was something."

"*A mystery!*" breathed Nancy, in an awestruck voice. "Oh, Miss Pollyanna!"

The next minute she was down at Pollyanna's side. "Tell me. It was after he found out ye was Miss Polly's niece that he didn't ever want to see ye again, wasn't it? And Miss Polly wouldn't send the jelly herself, would she?"

"No."

"And he began to act strangely after he found out ye was her niece, didn't he?"

"Why, y-yes, he did act a little odd," admitted Pollyanna, with a thoughtful frown.

Nancy drew a long sigh.

"Then I've got it, sure! *Mr. John Pendleton was Miss Polly Harrington's beloved!*" she announced.

"Why, Nancy, he couldn't be! She doesn't like him," objected Pollyanna.

"Of course she don't! *That's* the quarrel!"

Pollyanna looked doubtful. Nancy happily settled herself to tell the story.

"It's like this. Just before you come, Mr. Tom told me Miss Polly was in love once. I didn't believe it. But Mr. Tom said she was, and that her beloved was livin' now right in this town. And *now* I know, of course. It's John Pendleton."

Pollyanna *still* looked doubtful.

"Ain't he got a mystery in his life? Don't he shut himself up in that grand house alone, and never speak to no one? Didn't he act odd when he found out ye was Miss Polly's niece? And now ain't he owned up that ye remind him of somethin' he wants to forget? Why, Miss Pollyanna, it's as plain as the nose on yer face!"

"Oh-h!" breathed Pollyanna, in wide-eyed amazement. "But, Nancy, I should think if they loved each other they'd make up sometime. Both of 'em all alone all these years. I should think they'd be glad to make up!"

Nancy chuckled.

"Miss Pollyanna, it would be a pretty slick piece of business if you could *get* them to make up. Wouldn't folks stare some—Miss Polly and him! I guess, though, there ain't much chance!"

Pollyanna said nothing, but when she went into the house a little later, her face was very thoughtful.

CHAPTER NINE

Prisms

As the warm August days passed, Pollyanna went often to the great house on Pendleton Hill. But though the man sent for her frequently, when she was there he did not seem much happier.

She had twice tried to tell him about the "glad game." But neither time had she gotten beyond the beginning of what her father had said before John Pendleton turned the conversation to another subject.

Pollyanna never doubted now that John Pendleton was her Aunt Polly's one-time beloved. With all the strength of her heart, she wished she could bring happiness into their lonely lives.

Just how she was to do this, however, she could not see. She talked to Mr. Pendleton about her aunt. He listened, sometimes politely, sometimes irritably, often with a quizzical smile.

She tried to talk to her aunt about Mr. Pendleton, but Miss Polly would not listen. She always found something else to talk about. She also did that when Pollyanna was talking of others—Pollyanna's father, or Dr. Chilton, for instance. Aunt Polly seemed bitter against Dr. Chilton, as Pollyanna found out one day when a bad cold kept her shut up in the house.

"If you are not better by night I shall send for the doctor," Aunt Polly said.

"Then I'm going to be worse," Pollyanna laughed. "I'd love for Dr. Chilton to come see me!"

Aunt Polly blushed. "It will not be Dr. Chilton, Pollyanna," she said sternly. "Dr. Chilton is not our family physician. I shall send for Dr. Warren."

Pollyanna did not grow worse, however, and Dr. Warren was not summoned.

Early one morning, toward the end of August, Pollyanna called on Mr. Pendleton. It was then she found the flaming band of blue and gold and green edged with red and violet lying across his pillow.

Pollyanna stopped short in delight, clapping her hands together softly.

"Why, Mr. Pendleton, it's a baby rainbow!" she exclaimed. "Oh, how pretty it is! But how *did* it get in?"

John Pendleton laughed a little grimly. He was out of sorts with the world this morning.

"Well, I suppose it 'got in' through the edge of that glass thermometer in the window," he said wearily. "The sun *shouldn't* strike it at all but it does in the morning."

"Oh, but it's so pretty, Mr. Pendleton! And does just the sun do that? My! If it was mine I'd have it hang in the sun all day long!"

The man laughed. He was watching Pollyanna's intent face. Suddenly a new thought came to him. He touched the bell at his side.

"Nora," he said, when the elderly maid appeared at the door, "bring me one of the big brass candlesticks."

In a minute, a musical tinkling entered the room with Nora. It came from the glass pendants encircling the old brass candlestick in her hand.

"Thank you. You may set it here on the stand," directed the man. "Now get a string and fasten it to that window there. Let the string reach straight across the window from side to side. That will be all. Thank you," he said, when she had carried out his directions.

"Bring me the candlestick now, please, Pollyanna."

In a moment he was slipping off the pendants, one by one, until a dozen of them lay on the bed.

"Now, my dear, hook them to that little string Nora fastened across the window."

Pollyanna hung up three of the pendants in the sunlit window—and then saw what was going to happen. She was so excited she could scarcely control her shaking fingers enough to hang up the rest. But at last she was finished, and she stepped back with a low cry of delight.

The dreary bedroom had become a fairyland. Everywhere were bits of dancing red and green, violet and orange, gold and blue. The wall, the floor, and the furniture, even the bed itself, were aflame with shimmering bits of color.

"Oh, how lovely!" breathed Pollyanna. "How I would like to give them to Aunt Polly and Mrs. Snow and—lots of folks. I reckon *then* they'd be glad all right!"

Mr. Pendleton laughed.

"Oh, I forgot," Pollyanna said suddenly, "you don't know about the game."

"Suppose you tell me, then."

And this time Pollyanna told him. She told him the whole thing from the very first—from the crutches that should have been a doll. As she talked, she did not look at his face. Her eyes were still on the dancing flecks of color from the prism pendants swaying in the sunlit window.

"And that's all," she sighed. "And I think the sun is trying to play it—the game."

For a moment there was silence. Then Mr. Pendleton said in a low voice, "Perhaps. But I'm thinking that the very finest prism of them all is yourself, Pollyanna."

CHAPTER TEN

Surprises

Pollyanna entered school in September. She was well advanced for a girl of her years, and she was soon a happy member of a class of girls and boys her own age.

School, in some ways, was a surprise to Pollyanna. Pollyanna, certainly, was very much of a surprise to school. They were soon on the best of terms, however. Pollyanna confessed to her aunt that going to school *was* living, after all—though she had had her doubts before.

In spite of her delight in her new work, Pollyanna did not forget her old friends. She visited them as often as she could.

But John Pendleton did not seem satisfied. One Saturday afternoon, while they were sitting in the great library, he spoke to her about it.

"Pollyanna, how would you like to come and live with me?" he asked. "I don't see anything of you, nowadays."

Pollyanna laughed. Mr. Pendleton was such a funny man! "I thought you didn't like to have folks 'round," she said.

He smiled.

"Oh, but that was before you taught me to play that wonderful game of yours. Now I'm glad to be waited on, hand and foot!" He picked up one of the crutches at his side and playfully shook it at the little girl.

"Oh, but you aren't *really* glad at all for things. You just *say* you are," pouted Pollyanna. "You know you don't play the game right *ever*, Mr. Pendleton—you know you don't!"

The man's face grew suddenly very grave.

"That's why I want you around, little girl—to help me play it. Will you come live here?"

Pollyanna turned in surprise.

"Why, Mr. Pendleton, I can't. You know I can't. Why, I'm Aunt Polly's!"

Something crossed the man's face that Pollyanna could not quite understand. His head came up almost fiercely. But then he said gently, "Perhaps she *would* let you live here. Would you come, if she did?"

Now his voice was low and very sad.

"Pollyanna, long years ago I loved somebody very much. I hoped to bring her to this house. I pictured how happy we'd be together in our home all the long years to come."

"Yes," pitied Pollyanna, her eyes shining with sympathy.

"But I didn't bring her here. Never mind why. And ever since then this great gray pile of stone has been a house—never a home. It takes a woman's hand and heart, or a child's presence, to make a home, Pollyanna. I have not had either. Now will you come, my dear?"

Pollyanna sprang to her feet. Her face was fairly shining.

"Oh, Mr. Pendleton, you mean that you wish you had had that woman's hand and heart all this time?"

"Why, y-yes, Pollyanna."

"I'm so glad! Then it's all right," she sighed.

"Now you can take us both, and everything will be lovely. Aunt Polly isn't won over, yet. But I'm sure she will be if you tell it to her just as you did to me, and then we'd both come, of course."

A look of terror leaped to the man's eyes.

"Aunt Polly come—*here*?"

Pollyanna's eyes widened a little.

"Would you rather go *there*? Of course the house isn't quite so pretty, but it's nearer—"

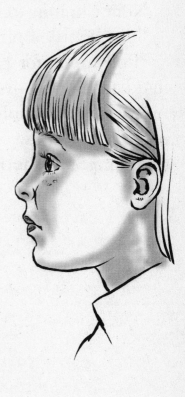

"Pollyanna, what *are* you talking about?" asked the man, very gently now.

"Why, about where we're going to live, of course," said Pollyanna, in surprise. "I *thought* you meant here, at first. You said it was here that you had wanted Aunt Polly's hand and heart all these years to make a home, and—"

The man raised his hand and began to speak, but the next moment he dropped it at his side.

Nora came in to announce: "The doctor, sir."

John Pendleton turned to Pollyanna quickly.

"Pollyanna, for Heaven's sake, say nothing of what I asked you—yet," he begged, in a low voice.

Pollyanna dimpled into a sunny smile. "Of course not! I know you'd rather tell her yourself!" she called back merrily over her shoulder.

CHAPTER ELEVEN

And More Surprises

The next Sunday morning, Dr. Chilton caught up to Pollyanna in his carriage as she was walking home from church.

"Let me drive you home, Pollyanna. I want to speak to you a minute. I was just driving over to your place. Mr. Pendleton sent a special request for you to see him this afternoon. He says it's very important."

Pollyanna nodded happily. "Yes, it is! I'll go."

The doctor's eyes twinkled. "I'm not sure I should let you go, young lady. Mr. Pendleton seemed upset from your last visit—and you're supposed to be his medicine."

Pollyanna laughed. "Oh, it wasn't me! It was my Aunt Polly!"

"Your—aunt?"

Pollyanna gave a happy bounce in her seat.

"Yes. And it's so exciting and lovely, just like a story, you know. I—I'm going to tell you. You see, he's in love with her—"

"Love!?" the doctor exclaimed.

"Yes," nodded Pollyanna happily. "That's the story part, you see. I didn't know it till Nancy told me. She said Aunt Polly had a beloved years ago—until they quarreled. Nancy did not know who it was, but now we do! It's Mr. Pendleton, you know."

The reins fell limp in the doctor's hands as the carriage pulled up to the Harrington house.

"Oh. No, I didn't know," he said quietly.

Pollyanna went over that afternoon to John Pendleton's house. He looked very nervous when the young girl arrived. He said at once, "Pollyanna, I've been trying all night to puzzle out what you meant about my wanting your Aunt Polly's hand and heart. What did you mean?"

"Why, because you were in love once. And I'm so glad you still feel that way now."

"In love!—Your Aunt Polly and I?"

Pollyanna opened her eyes wide.

"Why, Nancy said you were!"

The man gave a short laugh. "Well, I'm afraid Nancy didn't know."

"Then you weren't in love?" Pollyanna's voice was tragic with dismay.

"Never!"

"And it *isn't* all coming out like a book? Oh, dear! And it was all going so splendidly," sobbed Pollyanna. "I'd have been so glad to come—with Aunt Polly."

"And you won't—now?" The man asked the question without turning his head.

"Of course not! I'm Aunt Polly's."

The man turned now, almost fiercely.

"Before you were hers, Pollyanna, you were your mother's. And it was your mother's hand and heart that I wanted long years ago."

"My mother's?"

"Yes. I had not meant to tell you, but perhaps it's better that I do now."

John Pendleton's face had grown very white.

"I loved your mother, but she didn't love me.

She married your father. I did not know until then how much I did care. Since then I have been a cross, crabbed, unlovable, unloved old man—though I'm not even sixty yet. Then, one day you danced into my life and brightened my dreary old world with your cheeriness. I thought I never wanted to see you again, because I didn't want to be reminded of your mother. But now I want you always. Pollyanna, won't you come *now*?"

"But, Mr. Pendleton, there's Aunt Polly!" Pollyanna's eyes were blurred with tears.

"What about me? How do you suppose I'm going to be 'glad' about anything—without you? It's only since you came that I've been glad to live! But if I had you for my own little girl, I'd be glad for—anything. And all my money, to the last cent, would go to make you happy."

"Anybody with as much money as you have doesn't need *me* to make you glad about things," smiled Pollyanna. "You're making other folks so glad giving them things that you just can't help being glad yourself! Why, look at those prisms you gave Mrs. Snow and me, and the gold piece you gave Nancy on her birthday, and—"

"What gladness there was, was because of you. *You* gave those things, not I!" he said. "And that only goes to prove all the more how I need you, little girl." His voice softened. "If ever, ever I am to play the 'glad game,' Pollyanna, you'll have to come and play it with me."

The little girl's forehead puckered into a frown.

"All right. I'll ask Aunt Polly," she said wistfully. "I don't mean that I wouldn't like to live here with you, Mr. Pendleton, but... Well, anyhow, I'm glad I didn't tell her yesterday."

The sky was darkening fast into a thunder shower when Pollyanna hurried down the hill from John Pendleton's house. Halfway home she met Nancy with an umbrella.

"Miss Polly wanted me to come with this. She was *worried* about ye!"

"Was she?" murmured Pollyanna.

"You don't seem to notice what I said," Nancy said. "I said yer aunt was *worried* about ye! *You* don't seem to sense what it means to have Miss Polly *worried* about ye, child! It means she's at last gettin' somewheres near human. An' that she ain't jest doin' her duty by ye all the time."

"Why, Nancy," objected Pollyanna, "Aunt Polly always does her duty. She a very dutiful woman!"

Nancy chuckled, "You're right she is—and she always was, I guess! But she's somethin' more, now, since you came."

"There, that's what I was going to ask you, Nancy," Pollyanna sighed, with a frown. "Do you think Aunt Polly likes to have me here? Would she mind—if—if I wasn't here any more?"

"As if that wasn't jest what I was tellin' ye!" Nancy cried. "Didn't she send me quickly with an umbrella 'cause she seen a little cloud in the sky? Didn't she make me tote yer things downstairs, so you could have the pretty room you wanted? It's little ways that show how you've been softenin' her up—the cat, and the dog, and the way she speaks to *me*. There ain't no tellin' how she'd miss ye if ye wasn't here," finished Nancy.

"Oh, Nancy. You don't know how glad I am that Aunt Polly wants me!"

"As if I'd leave her now!" thought Pollyanna, as she climbed the stairs to her room a little later. "I always knew I wanted to live with Aunt Polly. But maybe I didn't know quite how much I wanted Aunt Polly to want to live with *me*!"

The task of telling John Pendleton her decision would not be an easy one, Pollyanna knew, and she dreaded it. As soon as she could, she hurried to his house, and found herself in the great dim library. John Pendleton sat near her, his long, thin hands on the arms of his chair, and his faithful little dog at his feet.

"Well, Pollyanna, is it to be the 'glad game' with me, all the rest of my life?" asked the man gently.

"Oh, yes," cried Pollyanna. "I've thought of the very gladdest kind of a thing for you to do, and—"

"Pollyanna, you aren't going to say no!" interrupted a voice deep with emotion.

Pollyanna turned away her eyes. She could not meet the hurt, grieved gaze of her friend.

"So you didn't even ask your aunt!"

"You see, I found out without asking. Aunt Polly *wants* me with her, and—and I want to stay, too," she confessed bravely. "You don't know how good she's been to me. Oh, Mr. Pendleton, I *couldn't* leave Aunt Polly now!"

There was a long pause. Only the snapping of the wood fire in the grate broke the silence. At last, however, the man spoke.

"No. I see. You couldn't leave her now."

"Oh, but there is the very gladdest thing you *can* do, truly there is!" Pollyanna reminded him. "You said only a woman's hand and heart or a child's presence could make a home. And I can get you a child's presence—not me, you know, but another one."

"As if I would have any but you!"

"But you will, when you know. You're so kind and good! And, you'll like Jimmy Bean. I know you'll take him!"

"Take—*who*?"

"Jimmy Bean. He's the 'child's presence,' you know, and he'll be so glad to be it!"

"Will he? Well, I won't," exclaimed the man. "Pollyanna, this is sheer nonsense!"

"You don't mean you won't take him? He'd be a lovely child's presence," faltered Pollyanna. She was almost crying now. "And you *couldn't* be lonesome—with Jimmy around."

"Pollyanna, I suspect you are more right than you know," he said gently. "In fact, I *know* that a 'nice live little boy' would be far better than being lonesome. Suppose you tell me a little more about this nice little boy."

Perhaps Jimmy Bean's sad, sweet story as told by Pollyanna's eager little lips touched a heart already strangely softened. For when Pollyanna went home that night, she carried with her an invitation for Jimmy Bean himself to call at Mr. Pendleton's great, stone house with Pollyanna the next Saturday afternoon.

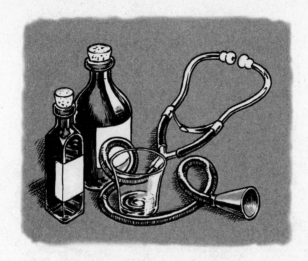

CHAPTER TWELVE

The Accident

At Mrs. Snow's request, Pollyanna went one day to Dr. Chilton's office to get the name of a medicine which Mrs. Snow had forgotten. As it chanced, Pollyanna had never before seen the inside of Dr. Chilton's office.

"I've never been to your home before! This *is* your home, isn't it?" she said, looking about her.

The doctor smiled a little sadly.

"Yes," he answered, "but it's a pretty poor apology for a home, Pollyanna. They're just rooms, that's all—not a home."

Pollyanna nodded her head wisely. Her eyes glowed with understanding.

"I know. It takes a woman's hand and heart, or a child's presence to make a home," she said. "Mr. Pendleton told me. Why don't you get a woman's hand and heart, Dr. Chilton? Or maybe you'd take Jimmy Bean—if Mr. Pendleton doesn't want him."

Dr. Chilton laughed.

"So Mr. Pendleton says it takes a woman's hand and heart to make a home, does he?" he asked curiously.

"Yes. Why don't you get a woman's hand and heart, Dr. Chilton?"

There was a moment's silence. Then very gravely the doctor said, "They're not always to be had for the asking, little girl."

Pollyanna frowned thoughtfully. Then her eyes widened in surprise.

"Why, Dr. Chilton, did you try to get somebody's hand and heart once, like Mr. Pendleton—and couldn't? Did you?"

The doctor got to his feet quickly and said, "Pollyanna, never mind about that now. Suppose you run back to Mrs. Snow. I've written down the name of the medicine. Was there anything else?"

Pollyanna shook her head as she turned toward the door.

It was on the last day of October that the accident occurred. Pollyanna, hurrying home from school, crossed the road at, she thought, a safe distance in front of a swiftly approaching car.

No one could tell afterward exactly what had happened, why it had happened, or who was to blame. But at five o'clock Pollyanna was carried, limp and unconscious, into her little room. There a white-faced Aunt Polly and a weeping Nancy undressed her tenderly and put her to bed. From the village, Dr. Warren was hurrying as fast as his car could bring him.

There appeared to be no bones broken, but the doctor looked very grave. He shook his head slowly and said that time alone could tell. A trained nurse was sent for. Aunt Polly's face grew even whiter. Nancy turned with a sob, and went back to her kitchen.

It was sometime the next morning that Pollyanna opened her eyes and realized where she was.

"Why, Aunt Polly, what's the matter? Isn't it daytime? Why don't I get up? Why, Aunt Polly, I can't get up," she moaned, falling back on the pillow. "What is the matter? Why can't I get up?"

Miss Polly's eyes looked up to the white-capped young woman standing in the window, out of the range of Pollyanna's eyes.

The young woman nodded.

"Tell her," the lips said.

Miss Polly cleared her throat, and tried to swallow the lump in her throat that would scarcely let her speak.

"You were hurt, dear, by an automobile last night. But never mind that now. Auntie wants you to rest and go to sleep again."

"Hurt? Oh, yes. I ran." Pollyanna's eyes were dazed. She lifted her hand to her forehead. "Why, it's bandaged and it hurts! Aunt Polly, I feel so funny, and so bad! My legs feel so strange—only they don't *feel* at all!"

Miss Polly struggled to her feet, and turned away. The nurse came forward quickly.

"Suppose you let me talk to you now," she began cheerily. "I am Miss Hunt, and I've come to help your aunt take care of you. And the very first thing I'm going to do is to ask you to swallow these little white pills for me."

Pollyanna's eyes grew a bit wild.

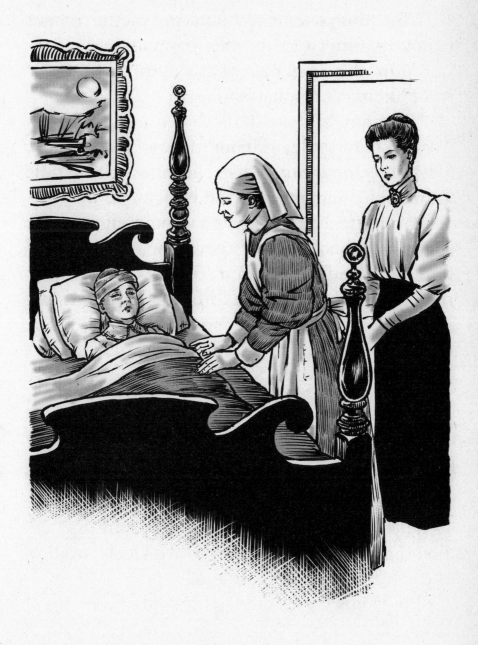

"But I don't want to be taken care of! I want to get up. Can't I go to school tomorrow?"

From the window where Aunt Polly now stood there came a half-stifled cry.

"Tomorrow?" smiled the nurse brightly. "Well, I may not let you out quite so soon as that, Miss Pollyanna. But just swallow these little pills for me, please, and we'll see what *they'll* do."

A minute later, Pollyanna spoke again. She spoke of school, and of the automobile, and of how her head ached. But very soon her voice trailed into silence as she drifted back into sleep.

CHAPTER THIRTEEN

A Woman's Hand and Heart

Pollyanna did not go to school next day or the day after that. But she did not realize this—or anything—very clearly until a week had passed. At last the fever went down, the pain lessened, and her mind awoke. She was then told again what had happened.

"So I am hurt, and not sick," she sighed at last. "Well, I'm glad of that."

"G-glad, Pollyanna?" asked her aunt who was sitting by her bed, holding her hand.

"Yes. I'd much rather have broken legs like Mr. Pendleton's than crippled ones like Mrs. Snow's. Broken legs get well, and crippled ones don't."

Miss Polly got suddenly to her feet and walked to the little dressing table across the room. Her face was white and drawn.

On the bed Pollyanna lay blinking at the dancing band of colors on the ceiling. It came from one of the prisms in the window.

"I'm glad it isn't smallpox, too," Pollyanna went on. "That would be worse than freckles. And I'm glad it isn't whooping cough or appendicitis or measles."

"You seem to be glad for a good many things, my dear," faltered Aunt Polly, putting her hand to her throat.

"I am." Pollyanna laughed softly. "I've been thinking of 'em—lots of 'em—all the time I've been looking up at that rainbow. I'm so glad Mr. Pendleton gave me those prisms. I'm glad of some things I haven't said yet. I don't know but I'm almost glad I was hurt."

"Pollyanna!"

Pollyanna laughed again. She turned bright eyes on her aunt. "Well, you see, since I have been hurt, you've called me 'dear' lots of times— and you didn't before. I love to be called 'dear.' Oh, Aunt Polly, I'm so glad you belong to me!"

Aunt Polly did not answer. Her hand was at her throat again. Her eyes were full of tears.

It was that afternoon that Nancy ran out to Old Tom, who was cleaning harnesses in the barn. Her eyes were wild.

"Mr. Tom, guess what's happened," she panted. "Who do you s'pose is in the parlor now with the mistress? It's—John Pendleton!"

Mr. John Pendleton did not have to wait long before a swift step warned him that Miss Polly was approaching. As he attempted to rise, she made a gesture of protest. She did not offer her hand, however, and her face was cold.

"I called to ask for—Pollyanna," he announced.

"Thank you. She is about the same," said Miss Polly. "Dr. Warren isn't quite sure what is wrong. He is in touch now with a New York specialist."

"But—but what *were* her injuries?"

"A slight cut on the head, one or two bruises, and an injury to the spine, which has seemed to cause paralysis from the hips down."

A low cry came from the man. There was a brief silence, then he asked, "And Pollyanna— how does she take it?"

"She doesn't know how things really are. She knows she can't move, but she thinks her legs are broken. She says she's glad it's broken legs like yours because broken legs get well. She talks like that all the time, until it seems as if I should die!"

It was this thought that made him ask very gently, as soon as he could control his voice, "I wonder if you know, Miss Harrington, how hard I tried to get Pollyanna to come and live with me. I wanted to adopt her."

Miss Polly relaxed a little. She thought what a brilliant future it would have meant for Pollyanna. She wondered if Pollyanna were old enough and selfish enough to be tempted by this man's money and position.

"I am very fond of Pollyanna," the man went on. "I am fond of her both for her own sake, and for her mother's. I was ready to give Pollyanna the love that I had held in for twenty-five years."

"*Love.*" With a sinking heart Miss Polly realized that this man had offered Pollyanna what she needed most—and what she herself had not given her. Love. She also realized how dreary her life would be without Pollyanna.

"Well?" she said.

The man smiled sadly. "She would not come," he answered. "She said you had been so good to her. She wanted to stay with you—and she said she *thought* you wanted her to stay."

He did not look toward Miss Polly. He turned his face toward the door. But instantly he heard a swift step at his side, and Miss Polly had put out her hand to grasp his warmly.

"When the specialist comes, and I know anything definite about Pollyanna, you will hear from me," said a trembling voice. "Good-bye—and thank you for coming. Pollyanna will be pleased."

Miss Polly sat with Pollyanna the next day and explained that another doctor would be coming to see her. A joyous light came into Pollyanna's eyes.

"Dr. Chilton! Oh, Aunt Polly, I'd so love to have Dr. Chilton! I'm so glad you do want him!"

Aunt Polly's face turned white, then red, then white again. But she tried to answer cheerily, "No, dear. It's a new doctor—a famous doctor from New York."

Pollyanna's face fell. And Aunt Polly's heart broke. She would do anything—anything but call Dr. Chilton—to please her dear Pollyanna.

And as the days passed, it did indeed seem that Aunt Polly was doing everything (but that) to please her niece. She brought in the cat and the dog to romp with Pollyanna on the bed. ("And she never done *that* before," remarked Nancy.) She dangled the prisms to make the light dance. ("It's as if her heart was just openin' up," Nancy told Old Tom.) And she wore her hair just as Pollyanna had once fixed it—with curls around her forehead. ("Why, she's *pretty*, she is, she is.")

Dr. Meade, from New York, did come to see Pollyanna. He examined her, then turned gravely to Dr. Warren. They left the room to speak.

Everyone said later that it was the cat that did it. Certainly, if Fluffy had not poked at Pollyanna's unlatched door, the door would not have swung open. And if the door had not been open, Pollyanna would not have heard her aunt's words.

In the hall the two doctors, the nurse, and Miss Polly stood talking. In Pollyanna's room Fluffy had just jumped to the bed with a little purr of joy. Then through the open door sounded clearly and sharply Aunt Polly's cry.

"Not that! Doctor, not that! You don't mean the child *will never walk again!*"

It was all confusion then. First, from the bedroom came Pollyanna's terrified "Aunt Polly! Aunt Polly!" Then Miss Polly realized that her words had been heard through the open door. She gave a low little moan, and—for the first time in her life—she fainted.

The nurse stumbled toward the open door. The two doctors stayed in the hall. Dr. Mead had caught Miss Polly, and Dr. Warren stood by helplessly as Pollyanna cried out again.

In Pollyanna's room, the nurse had found a gray cat on the bed purring up at a white-faced, wild-eyed little girl.

"Miss Hunt, please, I want Aunt Polly. I want her right away, quick, please! I want to know what she said just now. I want Aunt Polly to tell me 'tisn't true—'tisn't true!"

The nurse tried to speak, but no words came. Something in her face sent an added terror to Pollyanna's eyes.

"Miss Hunt, it is true! Oh! You don't mean I can't ever—walk again?

"There, there, dear—don't, don't!" choked the nurse. "Perhaps he didn't know. Perhaps he was mistaken. There are lots of things that could happen, you know. All doctors make mistakes sometimes. Don't think any more about it now— please don't, dear."

Pollyanna flung out her arms wildly. "But I can't help thinking about it," she sobbed. "Why, Miss Hunt, how am I to go to school, or to see Mr. Pendleton, or Mrs. Snow?" She sobbed wildly for a moment, then suddenly stopped and looked up.

"Why, Miss Hunt, if I can't walk, how am I ever going to be glad for—*anything*?"

"There, there, dear, just take this medicine," the nurse soothed. "By and by we'll be more rested, and we'll see what can be done then.

Things aren't half as bad as they seem, lots of times, you know."

Pollyanna took the medicine, and sipped the water from the glass in Miss Hunt's hand.

"Father used to say there was always something about everything that might be worse," Pollyanna said. "But I reckon he'd never just heard he couldn't ever walk again. I don't see how there *can* be anything that could be worse—do you?"

But the teary-eyed Miss Hunt could not trust herself to speak just then.

CHAPTER FOURTEEN

A Child's Presence

It did not take long for the entire town of Beldingsville to learn that the great New York doctor had said Pollyanna would never walk again. In kitchens and sitting rooms, and over backyard fences, women talked and wept. On street corners the men talked, too, and wept.

To Miss Polly's surprise, the Harrington home began to receive calls—calls from people she knew, and people she did not know: men, women, and children. Some brought books, bunches of flowers, or a food dish. Most wept. All asked about the little injured girl, and all sent her a kind message.

First came Mr. John Pendleton. He came without his crutches.

"I don't need to tell you how shocked I am," he began almost harshly. "But can nothing be done?"

Miss Polly gave a gesture of despair.

"Dr. Mead prescribed certain treatments and medicines that might help... But—he held out almost no hope."

"It seems cruel—never to dance in the sunshine again! My little prism girl!" John Pendleton rose abruptly, though he had just arrived. But at the door he turned.

"I have a message for Pollyanna," he said. "Will you tell her, please, that I have seen Jimmy Bean and—that he's going to be my boy hereafter. Tell her I thought she would be—*glad* to know. I shall adopt him, probably."

Miss Polly stood, silent and amazed, looking after the man who had just left her. Even yet she could scarcely believe what her ears had heard. John Pendleton, wealthy, independent, moody, reputed to be miserly and selfish, to adopt a little boy? And *such* a little boy!

With a somewhat dazed face, Miss Polly went upstairs to Pollyanna's room.

"Pollyanna, I have a message for you from Mr. Pendleton. He has just been here. He says to tell you he has taken Jimmy Bean for his little boy. He said he thought you'd be glad to know it."

Pollyanna's wistful little face flamed into sudden joy.

"Glad? *Glad?* Well, I reckon I am glad! Oh, Aunt Polly, I've so wanted to find a place for Jimmy, and that's such a lovely place! Besides, I'm so glad for Mr. Pendleton, too. You see, now he'll have the child's presence."

"The—what?"

Pollyanna blushed. She had forgotten that she had never told her aunt of Mr. Pendleton's wish to adopt her. And certainly she would not want to tell her now that she had ever thought for a minute of leaving her—this dear Aunt Polly!

"The child's presence," stammered Pollyanna hastily. "Mr. Pendleton told me once, you see, that only a woman's hand and heart or a child's presence could make a home. And now he's got it—the child's presence."

"Oh, I see," said Miss Polly very gently. She did see, more than Pollyanna realized. Her eyes were stinging with sudden tears for this caring child.

Pollyanna tried to change the subject.

"Dr. Chilton says so, too—that it takes a woman's hand and heart, or a child's presence, to make a home, you know," she remarked.

Miss Polly turned with a start.

"*Dr. Chilton*! How do you know—that?"

"He told me so."

Miss Polly did not answer. Her eyes were out the window.

"So I asked him why he didn't get 'em—a woman's hand and heart, and have a home."

"Pollyanna!" Miss Polly had turned sharply. Her cheeks showed a sudden color.

"Well, I did. He looked so—so sorrowful."

"What did he—say?" Miss Polly asked the question as if in spite of some force within her that was urging her not to ask it.

"He didn't say anything for a minute. Then he said very low that you couldn't always get 'em for the asking."

There was a brief silence. Miss Polly had turned again to the window. Her cheeks were quite pink.

Pollyanna sighed.

"He wants one, anyhow, I know, and I wish he could have one."

"Why, Pollyanna, *how* do you know?"

"Because, afterwards, on another day, he said that he'd give all the world if he did have one woman's hand and heart. Why, Aunt Polly, what's the matter?" Aunt Polly had risen hurriedly and gone to the window.

"Nothing, dear. I was changing the position of this prism," said Aunt Polly, whose whole face now was aflame.

CHAPTER FIFTEEN

The Game and Its Players

It was not long after John Pendleton's visit that Milly Snow called one afternoon. She blushed and looked very embarrassed when Miss Polly entered the room.

"I—I c-came to inquire for the—the little girl," she stammered.

"You are very kind. She is about the same. How is your mother?" asked Miss Polly wearily.

"That is what I came to tell Pollyanna," the girl said nervously. "After all she's done for mother—teaching her to play the game and all. We heard how now she couldn't play it herself. We thought if she could only know what she *had* done for us,

that it would *help*. She could be glad—that is, a little glad—" Milly stopped and waited for Miss Polly to speak.

"I don't think I quite understand, Milly. Just what is it that you want me to tell my niece?"

"You know nothing was ever right before for Mother. But now she lets me keep the shades up, and she takes interest in things. And she's actually begun to knit little things for fairs and hospitals. She's so *glad* to think she can do it.

"That was all Miss Pollyanna's doings," Milly went on. "She told Mother to be glad she had her hands and arms. That made Mother wonder why she didn't *do* something with her hands and arms. So she began to knit. We want you to please tell Miss Pollyanna that we understand it's all because of her. Maybe if she knew it, it would make her a little glad that she knew us. You'll tell her?"

These visits of John Pendleton and Milly Snow were only the first of many.

One day there was the Widow Tarbell.

"I'm a stranger to you, of course," she began at once. "But I'm not a stranger to your little niece, Pollyanna. I've been at the hotel all summer, and every day I've taken long walks for my health.

It was on these walks that I've met your niece. She's such a dear little girl! Her bright face and cheery ways reminded me of my own little girl that I lost years ago. I was so shocked to hear of the accident. The dear child! Will you just tell her that Mrs. Tarbell is glad now? I know it sounds odd, and you don't understand. But—if you'll pardon me, I'd rather not explain. Your niece will know just what I mean. Thank you, and pardon me, please, if I seem rude," she begged, as she left.

Miss Polly, by now confused, hurried upstairs to Pollyanna's room.

"Pollyanna, do you know a Mrs. Tarbell?"

"Oh, yes. I love Mrs. Tarbell. She's sick, and awfully sad, and she's at the hotel, and takes long walks. We go together. I mean—we used to." Pollyanna's voice broke, and two big tears rolled down her cheeks.

Miss Polly cleared her throat hurriedly.

"We'll, she's just been here, dear. She left a message for you—but she wouldn't tell me what it meant. She said to tell you that she's glad now."

Pollyanna clapped her hands softly.

"Did she say that—really? Oh, I'm so glad!"

"But, Pollyanna, what did she mean?"

"Why, it's the game, and—" Pollyanna stopped short, her fingers to her lips.

"What game?"

"N-nothing much, Aunt Polly. That is, I can't tell it unless I tell other things that I'm not to speak of."

Miss Polly wanted to question her niece further, but the distress on the little girl's face stopped the words before they were uttered.

Yet another visitor, a Mrs. Benton, showed up in her usual widow's black—but with a big blue bow at her throat.

"Will you tell the little girl I'm playing the game—and I've put on a bit of color?" she asked.

The door had scarcely closed behind her before Miss Polly went up to Nancy in the kitchen.

"Nancy, *will* you tell me what this 'game' is that the whole town seems to be babbling about? And what, please, has my niece to do with it?"

To Miss Polly's surprise and dismay, Nancy burst into tears.

"It means that ever since last June that blessed child has been makin' the whole town glad, an' now they're tryin' to make her a little glad, too. It's the game."

Miss Polly actually stamped her foot.

"There you go like all the rest. What game?"

"It's a game Miss Pollyanna's father learned her to play. She got a pair of crutches once when she was wantin' a doll. She cried like any child would. Her father told her that there was always somethin' to be glad about, an' that she could be glad about them crutches."

"Glad for *crutches*!" Miss Polly choked back a sob. She was thinking of the helpless little legs on the bed upstairs.

"Yes'm. He told her she could be glad 'cause she *didn't need 'em*. And after that he made a regular game of finding somethin' in everythin' to be glad about. And they called it the 'jest bein' glad' game. She's played it ever since."

"But why has she made such a mystery of it, when I asked her?"

Nancy hesitated.

"Beggin' yer pardon, ma'am, you told her not to speak of her father. She couldn't tell ye. 'Twas her father's game, ye see."

Miss Polly bit her lip.

"She wanted to tell ye, first off," Nancy went on, a little nervously. "She wanted somebody to play it with, ye know. That's why I begun it, so she could have someone."

"And these others?" Miss Polly's voice shook.

"Oh, almost everybody knows it now. Anyhow, I hear of it everywhere I go. Ye see, she's always wanted everybody to play the game with her."

"Well, I know somebody who'll play it now," choked Miss Polly, as she turned and sped through the kitchen doorway.

A little later, in Pollyanna's room, the nurse left Miss Polly and Pollyanna alone together.

"You've had another caller today, my dear," said Miss Polly quietly. "Do you remember Mrs. Benton? She came with a bright blue bow on."

Pollyanna smiled through tear-wet eyes.

"Did she? Did she, really? Oh, I am so glad!"

"Yes, she said she hoped you'd be. That's why she told you, to make you—*glad*, Pollyanna."

"Why, Aunt Polly, you spoke just as if you knew. *Do* you know about the game?"

"Yes, dear. Nancy told me. I think it's a beautiful game, and I'm going to play it now with you. Why, Pollyanna, I think all the town is wonderfully happier because one little girl taught people a new game."

Pollyanna clapped her hands. Then, suddenly, a wonderful light shone in her face.

"Why, Aunt Polly, there *is* something I can be glad about, after all. I can be glad I've *had* my legs, anyway—else I couldn't have done that!"

CHAPTER SIXTEEN

Through an Open Window

One by one the short winter days came and went. But they were not short to Pollyanna. They were long, and sometimes full of pain. But the little girl found ways to be cheerful. How could she not, with Aunt Polly playing the game now? Aunt Polly found *so* many things to be glad about! And, like Mrs. Snow, Pollyanna knitted wonderful things out of bright colored strings. She was glad she had her hands and arms, anyway.

Pollyanna saw people now, and always there were loving messages from those she could not see. They brought her something to think about— and Pollyanna needed new things to think about.

Once she had seen John Pendleton, and twice she had seen Jimmy Bean. John Pendleton had told her what a fine boy Jimmy was, and how well he was doing. Jimmy had told her what a first-rate home he had, and what bang-up "folks" Mr. Pendleton made. Both had said that it was all because of her.

The winter passed and spring came, but Pollyanna's treatment brought little change. There seemed every reason to believe that Pollyanna would never walk again.

Mr. John Pendleton, somewhat to his surprise, received a call one Saturday morning from Dr. Thomas Chilton.

"Pendleton," said the doctor, "I've come to you because you know about my... er... well, feelings for Miss Polly Harrington."

John Pendleton was taken aback. He did know that Miss Polly and Chilton had once been in love, but they had not talked of it for fifteen years.

"Pendleton, I want to see that child. I want to examine her. I *must* make an examination."

"Well—can't you?"

"*Can't* I? Pendleton, you know very well I have not been inside that door for over fifteen years.

Polly Harrington told me that the next time she *asked* me to enter it, I would know she was begging my pardon. It would mean everything would be as before—that she'd marry me. Perhaps you see her calling me now—but I don't!"

"If you're so anxious, couldn't you swallow your pride and forget the quarrel?"

"Forget the quarrel!" interrupted the doctor. "I'm not talking of that kind of pride. This is a case of sickness, and I'm a doctor. I can't butt in and say, 'Here, take me!' can I?"

"Chilton, what was the quarrel?"

"What's any lovers' quarrel after it's over?" Chilton snarled, pacing the room. "Never mind the quarrel! Pendleton, I must see that child. It may mean life or death. It will mean, nine chances out of ten, that Pollyanna Whittier will walk again!"

The words were spoken clearly, and they were spoken just as Dr. Chilton reached the open window near John Pendleton's chair. So it happened that a small boy kneeling beneath the window outside heard them.

Little Jimmy Bean sat up with ears and eyes wide open.

"Walk? Pollyanna?" John Pendleton was saying. "What do you mean?"

"I mean that her case is very much like one that a college friend of mine has just helped. For years he's been making this sort of thing a special study. I've kept in touch with him, and studied, too. I want to *see* the girl! But how can I, without a direct request from her aunt?"

"She must be made to ask you!"

"How?"

"I don't know."

Outside the window, Jimmy Bean stirred suddenly. Up to now, he had scarcely breathed.

"Well, by Jinks, *I* know how! I'll do it!" he whispered excitedly.

He crept around the corner of the house. Then he ran with all his might down Pendleton Hill to Miss Polly Harrington's house.

"It's Jimmy Bean. He wants to see ye, ma'am," announced Nancy in the doorway.

"Me?" asked Miss Polly, plainly surprised.

"Yes'm. He said it was you he wanted."

In the sitting room she found a round-eyed, flushed-faced boy, who began to speak at once.

"Ma'am, I suppose it's dreadful—what I'm doin', an' what I'm sayin', but I can't help it. It's for Pollyanna, an' that's why I come to tell ye that it's only pride that's keepin' Pollyanna from walkin'. I knew you *would* ask Dr. Chilton here if you understood."

"What? Jimmy, what are you talking about? Begin at the beginning, and be sure I understand each thing as you go. Don't plunge into the middle of it."

"Well, to begin with, Dr. Chilton come to see Mr. Pendleton, an' they talked in the library," Jimmy said. "Do you understand that?"

"Yes, Jimmy," Miss Polly said faintly.

"Well, the window was open, and I was weedin' the flowerbed under it. I heard 'em talk. Dr. Chilton knows some doctor that can cure Pollyanna, but he can't be sure till he *sees* her. But he told Mr. Pendleton that you wouldn't let him."

Miss Polly's face turned very red.

"But, Jimmy, I can't—I couldn't! That is, I didn't know!"

"Yes, an' I come to tell ye, so you *would* know," said Jimmy eagerly. "They said that you wouldn't let Dr. Chilton come. An' Dr. Chilton couldn't come himself, without you asked him, on account of pride. An' they was wishin' somebody could make you understand, only they didn't know who could. An' I was outside the window, an' I says to myself right away, 'By Jinks, I'll do it!' An' I come—an' have I made ye understand?"

Miss Polly turned her head from side to side. Jimmy, watching her with anxious eyes, thought she was going to cry. But she did not cry. After a minute she said brokenly, "Yes, Jimmy. I'll let Dr. Chilton see her. Now run home, Jimmy— quick! I've got to speak to Dr. Warren about bringing Dr. Chilton in. He's upstairs now. I saw him drive in a few minutes ago."

The next time Dr. Warren entered Pollyanna's room, a tall, broad-shouldered man followed close behind him.

"Dr. Chilton! Oh, Dr. Chilton, how glad I am to see *you*!" cried Pollyanna. And at the joy in her voice, more than one pair of eyes in the room brimmed with tears.

"It is all right, my dear, don't worry," soothed Miss Polly. "I told Dr. Chilton that I want him to look you over with Dr. Warren."

"Oh, then you asked him to come," murmured Pollyanna contentedly.

"Yes, dear, I asked him. That is—" And then Miss Polly's eyes met Dr. Chilton's eyes. They were filled with adoring happiness. With very pink cheeks, Miss Polly turned and left the room.

Over at the window the nurse and Dr. Warren were talking. Dr. Chilton smiled and held out both his hands to Pollyanna.

"Little girl, one of the very gladdest jobs you ever did has been done today," he said in a voice shaken with emotion.

At twilight, a wonderfully different Aunt Polly crept to Pollyanna's bedside. The nurse was at supper. They had the room to themselves.

"Pollyanna, dear, I'm going to tell *you* first of all. Someday Dr. Chilton will be your uncle. We're to be married. And *you* have made it all happen. Oh, Pollyanna, I'm so—glad!—darling!"

Pollyanna began to clap her hands.

"Oh, Aunt Polly, *you* were the woman's hand and heart he wanted so long ago! I knew you were! And that's what he meant by saying I'd done the gladdest job of all today. Why, Aunt Polly, I think I'm so glad that I don't mind even my legs, now!"

Aunt Polly swallowed a sob.

"Perhaps, someday, dear—" But Aunt Polly did not dare to tell yet the great hope that Dr. Chilton had put into her heart. She did say this, which was quite wonderful to Pollyanna's mind:

"Pollyanna, next week you're going to take a journey. On a nice comfortable little bed, you're going to be carried to a great doctor. He has a big house many miles from here for people with injured legs. He's a dear friend of Dr. Chilton's, and we're going to see what he can do for you!"

CHAPTER SEVENTEEN

A Letter from Pollyanna

Dear Aunt Polly and Uncle Tom,

Oh, I can—I can—I can walk! I did today all the way from my bed to the window! It was six steps. My, how good it was to be on legs again!

All the doctors stood around and smiled, and all the nurses cried. A lady who walked last week peeked into the door. Another one, who hopes she can walk next month, was invited to the party. She lay on my nurse's bed and clapped her hands. Even Tilly, who washes the floor, looked through the patio window. She called me 'Honey child' when she wasn't crying too much to call me anything.

I don't see why they cried. I wanted to sing and shout and yell! Oh—oh—oh! Just think, I can walk— walk—walk! Now I don't mind being here almost ten months. And I didn't miss the wedding, anyhow. Wasn't that just like you, Aunt Polly, to come here and get married right beside my bed, so I could see you. You always do think of the gladdest things!

Pretty soon, they say, I shall go home. I wish I could walk all the way there. I do. I don't think I shall ever want to ride anywhere any more. It will be so good just to walk. Oh, I'm so glad! I'm glad for everything. Why, I'm glad now I lost my legs for a while. For you never, never know how perfectly lovely legs are till you haven't got them—legs that go, I mean. I'm going to walk eight steps tomorrow.

With heaps of love to everybody,
—Pollyanna

THE END

ELEANOR H. PORTER

Eleanor Hodgman was born on December 19, 1868, in Littleton, New Hampshire. She did not spend much time in a formal school, since her family believed exploring the outdoors would teach her more.

She loved music and studied singing at the New England Conservatory of Music in Boston. She became a popular singer in concerts and church choirs in the area, and continued singing after she married John L. Porter, a businessman, in 1892.

In 1901, Eleanor became more interested in writing than in singing. She wrote short stories for magazines and newspapers. Her first popular book was *Miss Billy* in 1911, which had two sequels, followed by *Pollyanna* in 1913, and *Pollyanna Grows Up* in 1915. *Pollyanna* was a bestseller and inspired "glad clubs" all over the country and world. The book has also been made into a play and several movies.

Eleanor continued to write for the rest of her life, sometimes using the pen name of Eleanor Stuart. She died on May 21, 1920, in Cambridge, Massachusetts.